THE MAIDEN AND THE MARROW WITCH

A TALE OF MAGIC AND MURDER

REBECCA BUCHANAN

Copyright Rebecca Buchanan 2024.
All rights reserved.
This book or any portion thereof may not be reproduced or used in any manner whatsoever without the express written permission of the publisher except for the use of brief quotations in book reviews, blogs, or academic articles. This is a work of fiction. Names, characters, businesses, places, events, and incidents are either the products of the author's imagination or used in a fictitious manner. Any resemblance to actual persons, living or dead, or actual events is purely coincidental.

AI Training Prohibition: Unless otherwise noted, the author holds any and all exclusive rights to the entire content of this book, *The Maiden and the Marrow Witch: A Tale of Magic and Murder*. Any use of this publication to develop and "train" AI software in any way, for any reason, is expressly prohibited.

Gorgeous cover art by GetCovers.

 Created with Vellum

CONTENTS

*To the peoples of ancient Crete, whose art and creativity
continue to inspire;
And to the dedicated archaeologists who have uncovered so much
of that beauty*

~ ONE ~

"The Bull is dead."

In the wake of the Caretaker's announcement, silence filled the Hall of the Red Throne.

Ariemme bit the inside of her lip. The small movement was enough to send the golden bees in her hair to dancing, their faint tinkling the only sound within the red walls.

Outside, down the steps, beyond the pillars and silken curtains and chimes of shimmering glass, the people went on about their business: priests chanted and bled, fortunetellers peered into eyes and tossed bowls of teeth, and merchants shouted the worth and beauty of their wares in the first market of the day.

But inside ... inside there was silence and a terrible stillness.

Ariemme's eyes darted towards her mother.

The Pasithea sat upon her throne, bare-breasted, silken skirts pooling around her ankles and golden sandals, wreath of golden bees and bulls framing her head. Arrayed on her left, the venerable, the honored, the most skilled in the land: the Grandfather of Serpents, the

Master of Honey, and the Lorekeeper. The Shield stood at her back, bristling with knives, bronze armor glimmering, eyes hard. To the Pasithea's right, her dozen children, ranging in age from twenty summers to five, bare-chested and bare-breasted, their skirts each a different shade of red.

Tieffem stood closest to the Pasithea, only twelve years, their skirt a deep red; a match to their mother.

Ariemme, older by four years, stood at the far end of the line of children. Her skirt was so pale that it was pink. A pale pink.

The Pasithea broke the silence and the stillness with a sharp inhalation of breath and a single word. "How?"

The Caretaker remained standing, shoulders squared, hands clasped, unmoved by her anger. The collar of bull's horns — two, capped in gold and carved with images of plenty and virility — framed his neck and his grey-streaked beard. The points ended just above his heart, deliberately offset at a leftward angle to show his devotion and dedication to the Maiden's beloved Son.

"Magic, Holiness." The Caretaker's jaw flexed. "There can be no explanation other than malefic magic. A child of the Marrow Witch has done this."

Ariemme's eyes jumped between her mother and the Caretaker, but the Pasithea made no response except to tighten her jaw.

The Caretaker continued. "The Maiden's beloved Son was never out of sight of myself or one of my apprentices, in addition to the priests preparing for the sacrifice. There were also blessing-seekers, writing their prayers in blood upon the hides that will be burned along with the Bull."

The Grandfather of Serpents leaned forward as he spoke; straight-backed despite his age, a snake of vibrant green and purple curling around his arm and tasting the air. "And you are certain these were all true prayers?"

"I am. Each is inspected before the hide is removed, and a new one set in its place. And none of those hides were brought near to the Bull — and would not be until the sacrifice. It is impossible for a child of the Marrow Witch to have cursed and murdered the Bull in this way."

The Lorekeeper's veil rippled; all in white, and bare-footed; not even their eyes were visible. "Then the child of the Marrow Witch used the flesh or blood or bone of the Bull."

A moment of hesitation. "It would seem so, though ...."

The Pasithea scowled. "Speak."

The Caretaker tilted his chin. "Holiness, I have thoroughly examined the body of the Bull. There is no evidence of harm. None. No cuts. No bruises. No missing teeth. No nicks or shaving of his hooves or horns."

"You are saying that the body of the Bull is perfect?"

"I am, Holiness. The Bull is dead. Only a child of the Marrow Witch could have slain him. But I cannot see — I cannot explain — *how*."

The Pasithea rose slowly to her feet, silken skirts swinging as she moved forward a single step. Her crown of bees and bulls glimmered. The Grandfather of Serpents and the Master of Honey and the Lorekeeper all watched her, still, while the Shield moved forward, matching her steps.

"You have failed in your sacred duty, Caretaker. You will find this child of the Marrow Witch and you will present them at the time of sacrifice. They have slain the Maiden's beloved Son. Their blood must be shed in punishment and atonement. And if not the Marrow Witch's malicious child ...." The Pasithea tilted her head, waiting.

The Caretaker straightened his shoulders, lifted his

chin, echoing her words. "I am the Caretaker and I have failed in my sacred task. If I fail again, then I offer myself in the bull's place. Freely and willingly."

A curt nod from the Pasithea. "You have until the sun settles beyond the edge of the world."

The Caretaker bowed. Despite his words, Ariemme could see his knees shaking.

The Pasithea turned and strode from the room, through the archway towards her private quarters, her skirts sweeping across the stone. The guards flanked her, and the Shield followed; then Tieffem, one brow raised in contempt and frustration; then the Grandfather of Serpents and the Master of Honey; then Ariemme's siblings, reddest skirt to pale red to pink.

Only Ariemme stayed, and the Caretaker, and — oddly — the Lorekeeper.

Their veiled head swung towards Ariemme, but it was impossible to see the direction of their eyes through the cloth.

"Where will you go?"

Ariemme tightened her shoulders when she realized that she had spoken aloud. Her question was too noisy in the nearly empty Hall of the Red Throne, echoing from the pillars and the stone floor.

For a long moment, the Caretaker did not seem to hear her. His shoulders twitched, his hands dropping to his sides. Finally, he answered. "I ... will begin with my apprentices. The priests. I shall question them again. Perhaps I shall catch one in a lie, or ... perhaps one of them saw something strange, out of place, and will remember."

Ariemme crossed the stones to him, her bare feet silent. The golden bee ornaments that capped the ends of her braids clicked gently.

He looked down at her.

Your eyes are too much like his. Your nose and cheekbones. There is too much of him in you, and not enough of me. The Pasithea had sighed. *I should have chosen a man with weaker seed, but I liked those eyes.*

"I shall assist you."

The Caretaker chuckled, for a moment the grimness of his expression replaced with affection and indulgence. "I treasure your offer. But it is Vernaltide. You are a child of the Pasithea, and you have your own tasks to prepare for the rite this evening."

Ariemme flinched.

"Do not despair yet." He lightly touched her cheek. "There is time. I may yet find this child of the Marrow Witch."

With that he turned away, descending the stairs outside the Hall and disappearing into the early morning sun.

Too much of him in you. Your skirt will never be red.

"He will die."

Ariemme jumped. She had completely forgotten that the Lorekeeper still remained in the Hall. She turned to find the white-robed figure only three steps away. Their sleeves drooped, hiding their hands, and their skirts covered their feet. They looked like one of the unpainted statues of the Wavemaker in the Hall of Potters.

But then it was the Wavemaker who had first given the people the Lore, who had blessed the first keeper to hold it safe and speak it true.

Ariemme tightened her jaw. "He did not murder the Bull."

"No." The veil barely fluttered. "But there must be a sacrifice. The Maiden must know our gratitude, and we must understand the horrors from which our people escaped. In years and ages past, when there was no perfect Bull, others offered themselves in place of the beloved Son. On three separate Vernaltides, it was a child of the Pasithea — grown into their mind and body — who carried the people's blessings and entreaties to the Maiden."

"You think I would — should — take my sire's place?"

The Lorekeeper tilted their head. "You *are* the least-favored of your mother's children. And a resentful heart is easily corrupted. Perhaps we should be looking to *you* as the child of the Marrow Witch."

Ariemme's heart stuttered in her chest. "What? … How?"

"Your dislike of your sibling is well-known. They, after all, can speak with the bees and the bulls, call the rains, feel the cracking of the earth deep down. They are the most powerful of the Pasithea's children. It is they who will inherit the Red Throne, not you."

Ariemme laughed. It was a harsh sound.

"I have no wish for the Red Throne, Lorekeeper. I never have. And, as you say, I am the weakest of my mother's children. Were I to sit upon the Throne, it would be the doom of our people. If the Pasithea cannot speak with the bees and the bulls, call the rains, or feel the cracks of the earth before they tear down our buildings and turn back the tides — well, they are no Pasithea."

Silence.

Outside, down the steps, beyond the pillars and silken curtains and chimes of shimmering glass, Ariemme could hear the priests chanting, fortunetellers tossing bowls of teeth, and merchants and shoppers haggling as the first market of the day drew to an end.

Suddenly embarrassed, she crossed her arms and

looked away. Down. Stared at her toes curling against the stone.

"Come."

She lifted her head, eyes wide as the Lorekeeper turned in a swirl of white and moved towards the far right corner of the Hall.

Confused, still embarrassed, Ariemme scampered to catch up.

The Lorekeeper was quick, moving between the great pillars to the door in the corner. They pushed it open and strode down the corridor. Narrow windows let in the morning sunshine, illuminating the paintings of dolphins and fish, gryphons and flowers.

"Tell me the story, child of the Pasithea. Recite for me the origins of the first covenant, and the origins of the second covenant. Recite for me the Lore of the Bull."

Ariemme swallowed, calling the sacred tale to mind. *Speak! Just say the words!*

"Long ago, the people lived in a land consumed by the bloodlust of the Marrow Witch. They knew nothing of the Maiden, or even the Wavemaker. They knew only the greed of the Marrow Witch. Fires burned on every mountaintop. Grandparents were stolen from their beds, children stolen from their parents' arms, blood and breath stolen for malefic magic. The bones piled high, nearly eclipsing the sun. Widows and orphans cried out in fear and despair, and the Maiden heard them. The Maiden appeared to them, and told them to build ships, many ships, enough to carry all those who despaired. They built their ships and fled, following the song of the Wavemaker across the sea. They found this island, a land with no name, a land of bees and bulls and plenty. The Maiden appeared again. From among the people, she chose one. The first Pasithea, the first to hear the bees and the bulls, to call the rain, to feel the cracking of the earth. And the Maiden said that this nameless land would be ours, unto forever. The first covenant."

The Lorekeeper turned a sharp corner, moving deeper into the Hall of the Pasithea. The windows disappeared, replaced by golden-white torches. "Continue, child."

She cleared her throat. "Unto forever. But under one condition."

Another turn, this time down a flight of stairs. There were fewer torches here.

Ariemme had never been in this part of the building.

"Continue."

"Ah, yes." Ariemme lifted her skirts, golden bees clicking and clacking as she bounced down the stairs behind the Lorekeeper. "That blood must be shed *only* in Her honor, and that it must be freely given."

The stairs ended, opening onto a narrow passage. It was barely wide enough for the Lorekeeper to walk straight. If the Shield had been leading the way, he would have had to turn sideways.

"And did the people hear the words of the Maiden?"

"Yes. Generations passed. Peaceful. The people created farms and granges and vineyards and apiaries and orchards, raised bulls and sheep and goats, fished in the waters of the Wavemaker. But then, one day, twins were born. Sons of the Pasithea."

Ariemme's feet slowed, feeling the darkness all around, the weight of the stones and earth. Her body grew cold.

Where was the Lorekeeper taking her?

"Continue, child. Pay attention to what you have just said, and to what you are about to say."

Ariemme stopped, frowning.

The Lorekeeper stopped, too, turning back to face her.

At least, Ariemme assumed the Lorekeeper was facing her. They were a shadowy white blur down here, in the depths beneath the Hall of the Pasithea.

"The younger twin was especially beloved by the Maiden," she continued. "Not only could he speak with the bees and the bulls, call the rains, and feel the cracks in the earth, but he could read the patterns of the stars and clouds, sing in the language of the gryphons, and swim with the dolphins in the waters of the Wavemaker.

"The elder twin was jealous. And, in his anger and hate, he sought out the Marrow Witch herself, and a curse by which he might slay his brother."

Ariemme paused, mind churning.

The Lorekeeper waited.

"The Marrow Witch promised the elder brother what he most desired: a curse to kill his brother. She required only one thing: his blood ...."

"But," the Lorekeeper prompted.

"But it was a trick." Ariemme took a hesitant step towards the shadowed white blur. "The elder shed his blood willingly, yes, but not in honor of the Maiden. He broke the first condition of the first covenant. And ... oh ...." Ariemme's eyes widened in the dark. She pressed shaking fingers to her lips. "*Twins.*"

The Lorekeeper nodded once and turned away, making their way down the corridor again.

Ariemme hastened to catch up, her words even faster than her steps. "They were *twins*. The brothers, the sons of the Pasithea, they were twins. Blood alike. When the elder gave his blood to the Marrow Witch and she created the curse and he cast that curse, he killed his brother — but he also killed *himself*."

Without breaking their stride, the Lorekeeper reached

out and pushed against the wall. The stone moved smoothly to one side, making only the barest scraping sound. They stepped through, Ariemme nearly trodding on the hem of their white robes.

She stopped in surprise, gaping at the room that spread out before her.

They had come out on a balcony, framed on the far side by narrow red pillars and a low curved wall. There was a wooden table here, polished and smoothed by age and use. Padded benches and chairs crowded around the table. And a great chandelier with dozens upon dozens of candles hung over the center of the table, filling the balcony with warm light.

Stairs at either end of the balcony led down in a swooping arc.

Ariemme took a few hesitant steps, moving to the low wall. The golden bees in her hair clicked and clacked softly.

She peered out into the space below.

The walls of the cavern were untouched, rough and striated; even cracked in a few places, the crevices as wide as her arm. Only the floor had been smoothed out, but even then eruptions of grey-black rock here and there created natural hills and outcroppings. The smooth spaces were covered in shelves and cubbies and cabinets and trunks, each filled with neatly labelled and tagged scrolls. More chandeliers hung from the rough ceiling, enough to illuminate the entire Lore Room.

For this could be nothing else.

"I didn't know. I had no idea that the Lore Room was real."

The Lorekeeper moved up beside her, hands tucked deep into their sleeves. "It is not. There is no Lore Room.

The Lore given to us by the Wavemaker is never written down, only spoken."

Ariemme frowned, lifting a shaking hand towards the cavern. "Than this is …?"

The Lorekeeper seemed to shrug. "Histories. Records. Births and deaths. Reports of the fishing fleet and honey harvests. Shopping lists and kitchen orders. Every piece of paper, every piece of writing that has passed into or out of the Hall of the Pasithea has been preserved here. If it becomes too old and fragile, the words are re-written and saved. All the way back to the first Pasithea named by the Maiden." The Lorekeeper tilted their head down at Ariemme. "I believe that we shall find what we seek here."

Ariemme bit the inside of her lip. "You believe the Bull had a twin. And that the child of the Marrow Witch cursed and killed the twin, thereby cursing and killing the Maiden's beloved Son, as well."

"I do."

"But that would have been a lie. A deceit committed upon the Pasithea herself and all of the people."

A nod, the veil rippling. "Precisely. When the second covenant was established, the Maiden demanded the Vernaltide sacrifice of a bull — a reminder of the horrors of blood and fire that we left behind, that could stain the land again if we fall to the lust and greed of the Marrow Witch."

"And it was decreed that no twinned bulls would be offered up *precisely* because they could be killed in this way."

A second nod, the Lorekeeper's voice warm with approval. "Exactly. So, was the lie deliberate, or born of pride or ignorance? Perhaps this was the plan of the child of the Marrow Witch all along. To interfere with the sacrifice, the foundation of the second covenant, and thereby earn the Maiden's wrath and ire."

"Or … or perhaps the granger who bred the Bull wanted so badly for it to *be* the sacrifice that they lied and hid the existence of the twin." Ariemme twisted her fingers around the top of the wall, gaze moving slowly around the massive cavern. Now that she looked, she could see the Lorekeeper's three apprentices walking among the cabinets and cubbies and trunks. "Or perhaps the person who bought the Bull and traveled with it to the Hall as a potential sacrifice was unaware that it had a twin."

"Very good. Well reasoned." The Lorekeeper waved a hand towards the labyrinth of scrolls. "Shall we begin?"

~ TWO ~

There was no sense of the passing of time, not down here in this cavern far beneath the Hall of the Pasithea. Ariemme knew that she had only until the setting of the sun. If the child of the Marrow Witch was not found, then the Caretaker — he who had lain with her mother — would be sacrificed in place of the Bull.

And, if the Maiden was willing, she would accept that sacrifice and the second covenant would hold true for another year, and the people and the island would prosper.

She had accepted human offerings before, given willingly when there was no perfect Bull.

Perhaps she would again.

Perhaps.

Ariemme lifted onto her toes, squinting at the tags that dangled from the ends of a bundle of scrolls. The cubby was filled near to overflowing. Actually, this entire cabinet of cubbies nearly overflowed with ... yes. Records of purchases of bull calves. The Pasithea did not care who bought or sold how many chickens or goats or sheep or pigs. But the sales of all bulls and bees had to be noted and reported to the

13

Hall, and these cubbies were filled with reports dating back twenty years.

At least they were in chronological order.

The Bull that had been deemed perfect and selected as the Maiden's beloved Son had only been three years of age. Ariemme had occasionally visited the pens maintained by the Caretaker and his apprentices, but she seemed to recall that the bull who was eventually chosen had been there for about six months; along with a dozen other candidates.

So the Bull would have been delivered sometime around the past Autumntide.

Ariemme walked her fingers across the scrolls, eyes skimming the tags until she found the one from the previous autumn. She carefully shifted it loose, trying not to knock over the other scrolls. Finally, she was able to move back and unroll it.

It was as wide as her arm span, but not very long. Eight columns filled the page from top to bottom. The date of the bull's arrival at the pens; the grange where the bull originated; the bull's age; the sire and dam, if known (a surprising number of those were blank); the determination of the Caretaker (yea or nay); and the amount of coin, honey, or other goods traded for the bull if it was accepted. The last column was for bull deaths from natural causes or accidents.

Only twenty-seven bulls had been brought before the Caretaker last autumn. Of those, twenty had been rejected. Of the seven that the Caretaker accepted, one had died when it was stupid enough to remain outside during a winter freeze, and another had been gored badly in a fight and died of infection.

That left five.

The bull that had been eventually selected as the Maiden's beloved Son had to be among these five.

"You have found something?"

Ariemme looked up as the Lorekeeper appeared at her side, then back down at the thick ink scribbles and columns. "Possibly. Where are the records of the bull births?"

The Lorekeeper waved a hand and led Ariemme down a row of shelves, in and around the silent apprentices, around a protrusion of grey-black rock, to a fat four-sided column. The diamond-shaped cubbies that covered the column from top to bottom were filled with more scrolls, but these were much wider and longer than the one Ariemme still held.

There were more bulls birthed than were ever brought before the Caretaker.

The Lorekeeper looked down at her expectantly.

"Oh, yes." Ariemme cleared her throat. "Five bulls. They were born on the Grange of the Red Clover, the Grange of the Double-Striped Bee, the Grange of the Still Pond, the Grange of the Broken Horn, and ... the Grange of the Cork Tree."

Quickly and efficiently, the Lorekeeper selected the appropriate scrolls and handed them all to Ariemme. Her arms full, she followed the Lorekeeper back to the far end of the cavern, up the stairs, to the table in the middle of the balcony.

Under the warm light of the chandelier, Ariemme laid out the purchase record beside the scrolls of birth records.

Three bulls had been born at the Red Clover at the right time to possibly have been selected for the sacrifice. Only one bull each had been born at the Double-Striped Bee and the Still Pond, while two had been born at the Broken Horn and the Cork Tree.

Ariemme ground her teeth. "This would be easier if the bulls were given some sort of unique designation. A number, perhaps. Or an alphanumeric code."

"Some combination of their home grange, year of brith, and year of acceptance by the Caretaker?"

"Yes, yes, exactly." Ariemme nodded, bees clicking, then stumbled to a halt. "Um. I apologize, Lorekeeper. I did not mean to insult your practices, your method of record keeping, which date all the way back …."

But the Lorekeeper was waving one hand in a placating, dismissive gesture. "Nonsense. Your idea is sound. I shall discuss it with the Grandfather of Serpents, the Master of Honey, and the Caretaker, and see that it is instituted — when this is over, of course."

Ariemme's lips worked soundlessly. She dipped her head. "Thank you, Lorekeeper. I am honored." When there was no response she cleared her throat and turned back to the records spilled across the table. "The bulls from the Granges of the Double-Striped Bee and the Still Pond were single births from small herds. The Grange of the Red Clover, on the other hand, is large; almost five hundred head. And three bulls were born there at the right time. It would have been easy to hide a twin birth."

"And the others?"

Ariemme bent closer to the scrolls, fingers tracing over the ink, comparing dates. "Also smaller granges. Broken Horn and Cork Tree have fewer than thirty head of cattle each. Two bulls were born at each grange at the right time, but …. Oh. That's …." Her voice trailed off.

"Yes? What?"

Ariemme's eyes darted from the Lorekeeper to the scroll

and back again. "One of the bulls, born at the Grange of the Cork Tree, *was* a twin. But the bull's twin died only a week after the birth." She paused, mind turning. She drew a breath, holding very still. "Lorekeeper?"

"Yes?"

She paused again, trying to find the right words. She turned slightly and found that the Lorekeeper was seated in one of the plush chairs now. "Would the twin have to be *alive* for the curse to affect the Maiden's beloved Son?"

The Lorekeeper tilted their head, and Ariemme got the distinct impression that they were smiling. "Alive, no. Well-preserved, yes."

"So ... it is possible that the child of the Marrow Witch learned that the Beloved son of the Maiden was a twin. And learned where the corpse of the deceased twin was buried. And used some uncorrupted part of the corpse — the bones, perhaps, or some of the hide — it has only been three years — much of the body would be left intact — to craft the curse."

The Lorekeeper was nodding slowly. "And thus no mark was left upon the Maiden's beloved Son."

"Did you ...?" Ariemme felt her eyes narrow. "Did you *know*? Did you know this is how the child of the Marrow Witch attacked?"

"I suspected." The Lorekeeper waved a hand towards the railing and the labyrinthine archive beyond. "I spend much of my time studying our history, our poetry, our arcane texts. Even the few scrolls that were brought across the sea with the first settlers."

Ariemme swallowed hard, the golden bees in her hair clicking. "I did not know there were such texts."

The Lorekeeper seemed to shrug. "There are many things you do not know. Many things you could come to know, if you so choose." They tapped a finger on the Caretaker's purchase record; their skin was wrinkled, the nail beginning to yellow with age. "But there are other things you must come to know first."

"The location of the twin's corpse. If it was well-preserved enough to create the curse. And the identity of the child of the Marrow Witch."

"It is nearing high sun. And the sun will set during the seventh hour after high sun. I believe the Grange of the Cork Tree is located in the south-eastern portion of the Domain of the Golden-Clawed Gryphon. A fast horse should get you there in ... two hours?" They leaned back, settling against the plump cushions. "I suggest you pack your lunch and eat it on the way."

~ THREE ~

SHE WOULD NEED MORE THAN A LUNCH.

A child of the Marrow Witch.

Ariemme suppressed a shudder as she made the long, back and forth, back and forth climb up from the archives to the Hall of the Pasithea. Rough natural rock and darkness gave way to smooth, polished stone and high windows filled with sunlight. The faint scent of bread, oranges, honey, and roasting meat touched her nose.

She had no magic of her own; or, very little, at any rate. She could not commune with the bees and the bulls, summon the rains, or feel the deep down cracking of the earth. She did not even possess lesser abilities, such as curving the wind, dancing with water, or walking with fire. She could talk to snakes (a little) and understood bird song (a little). But not enough to apprentice with the Grandfather of Serpents or join the choir of Gryphon Singers who heralded the changes of the seasons from the mountain peaks.

Her skirt was pale pink, and it would remain pale pink. Never red.

How could she possibly find and defeat a child of the Marrow Witch?

"Sister, what have you been about?"

Ariemme skipped to a stop, gaze refocusing on Tieffem. Her sibling stood in front of her, a head shorter, scowling up at her, their arms crossed.

"Mother has noted your absence," the Heir continued. "She is expecting you to attend upon her, and prepare for the Vernaltide rites."

Ariemme straightened her back, tongue working as she hunted for the right words.

Tieffem was correct. She should report to the Pasithea, tell her what had been discovered in the archives, tell her that soldiers needed to be sent to the Grange of the Cork Tree.

But then there would be questions, and more questions. And the Lorekeeper would be summoned and the records would be analyzed and there would be yet more questions and debate and —

Too much time. Time she did not have.

Time the Caretaker did not have.

(And what if the Maiden rejected the Caretaker's sacrifice? It was the child of the Marrow Witch who should die this sunset, unwillingly, yes, but a justified sacrifice. Surely the Maiden would understand, and accept, and the second covenant would hold true.)

Tieffem scowled harder, foot tapping against the stone. A gust of wind through the high windows sent their red skirt to dancing around their ankles.

But the Lorekeeper had not told Ariemme to report any of this to the Pasithea. They had just told her to pack a lunch.

"I will explain all to Mother when I return." Ariemme

twisted and stepped around her sibling, continuing down the corridor. "Tell her I will be back for the sunset rites — and that I will bring the true sacrifice with me."

Tieffem ran after her. "What do you mean, sister? The Caretaker has consented to assume the Bull's place."

"Nay. He shall not. He is not responsible. It is the murderer who shall die this night."

Tieffem was silent, their sandals clapping against the stone.

Ariemme hastened her steps, making for the heavy wooden door at the end of the hallway. Down the exterior stairs, and she would find herself in the interior courtyard beside the kitchens. Then across the courtyard, down another corridor, another short flight of stairs, and she would be at the stables in an exterior courtyard on the south side of the Hall of the Pasithea.

"You know the name of the child of the Marrow Witch? You know who has forsaken the covenant and betrayed the Maiden?"

"I — no. But I know how they cursed and murdered the Bull." Ariemme shoved the door open and blinked painfully. It was brighter out here, at high noon, than it had been in the corridor. Moving by memory, she released the door and made her way down the stairs. Her vision cleared after a few steps and she turned to find Tieffem still following her, their expression changed from one of irritation to one of determination.

"I will accompany you."

Ariemme gaped at her sibling. Her toes caught and she nearly fell, only saving herself by dragging her hand along the stone wall. Her palm stung and she shook her hand, grimacing. "Absolutely not."

She ignored Tieffem's "Absolutely yes" and hastened down to the interior courtyard.

The space was filled with chefs and apprentice chefs and bakers and apprentice bakers and butchers and apprentice butchers, standing still and running around, shouting and whispering and muttering. Some held knives, others great spoons or brushes. Some stood at tables or stone ovens, others over bubbling vats or beside carcasses half-skinned, the meat and fat glistening in the sun. Some carried trays and platters, others huge amphorae and jugs, still others the skins of rabbits and sheep and goats bound for the furriers and vellum-makers.

The kitchen courtyard was as much a labyrinth as the archives far below.

And Ariemme knew it as well as she knew her own room.

She dove among the tables and ovens and bubbling vats, twisting around harried apprentices and screaming chefs. She grabbed an orange from one table, scooped up a loaf of bread from another. Tieffem disappeared among the crowd, yelling her name. She ignored them and hauled a small packet of dried fish off another table, then a wineskin off the platter of a startled apprentice. A hunk of cheese was last, just before the chef could chop it in half, the cleaver whistling past her fingers.

Juggling her lunch, the wineskin over one shoulder, Ariemme made for one of the doors on the far side of the courtyard.

Through the door, the sounds and scents of the kitchens mostly lost behind her as she trotted along.

Then the door opened and Tieffem was at her back again. She could hear the scowl in their voice.

"I am the Heir. If there is a threat to the land and the covenant, I should accompany you."

Through another door and down a short flight of stairs, right to the stables. Stalls for the horses occupied three sides of the courtyard, while the fourth stood wide open, delicately carved columns and plinth marking the gateway. She could smell the animals, and hay and apples and carrots; hear the neighing and whuffing, and the soothing words of the stablehands.

"Yes, you are the Heir." The right words, for once, came easily. "If there is a threat to the land and the covenant, *you* should be the one to report it to the Pasithea."

Someone had left a cotton sheet to dry on a bale of hay. Ariemme grabbed it as she went, tossing her food in the middle, twisting and tying it, looping the bundle over her shoulder.

She tested the weight and balance, wineskin on one side, food on the other.

That would do.

Now, for a mount. She needed a fast horse, one with stamina. Steady, calm, but quick. Not like the usual animals she took for sedate rides around the city, or on tours of the island with the Pasithea.

No, not Sunrise Cloud. Not Seamist, either. Another stall, another.

Tieffem was still arguing.

"You assume too much authority, sister. This is a matter for the Pasithea and her council, not ... *you.*"

Pale pink. Not red.

Jaw tight, Ariemme continued down the line of stalls. She ignored the curious looks of the stablehands, ignored her sibling, ignored the tightness in her belly.

Ah. This one.

Sparrow Song.

She flipped the latch, taking the bridle that hung to the side and slipping it over the horse's head. Sparrow Song lipped at her hand and stepped calmly from his stall.

Ariemme dragged over a mounting block with one foot. She braced her hands and swung onto the horse's bare back, shifting into a more comfortable position so that her wide skirt hiked up around her knees.

"This *is* a matter for me, Tieffem. It is my home that is threatened, as much as yours. And he is *my* father."

A touch of her heels, a click of her tongue, and Sparrow Song leaped away, through the gate, and down the street. South to the Grange of the Cork Tree and the corpse of the bull.

***

They went slowly at first, so slowly that she was grinding her teeth in frustration, navigating the densely crowded streets of the capital: pilgrims carrying flails made of cow tails and necklaces of cow teeth, merchants hefting beautifully carved horns and amphorae filled with honey, fortunetellers half-drunk on blood-mead, bards starting songs and then demanding coins to finish.

Once the masses of celebrants finally cleared, though, and they passed from the city proper and into the agricultural lands, she let Sparrow Song run free, and he did not disappoint. With a delighted whinny, the horse sprinted down the road, kicking up shiny white gravel. Faster and faster. She laughed, hands tight around the bridle, the wineskin and bundle of food banging against her sides.

When they reached the first crossroads, brightly painted signs pointing in five different directions, Ariemme turned south-east. She slowed Sparrow Song to a cooling trot, then a walk. She took a heavy gulp of the wine and tore off some of the bread. The sun was hot against the top of her head and her shoulders and her bare chest and back.

When the horse had recovered, she let him run again. He tossed his head, his mane snapping, his hooves skimming the road.

An hour passed. Merchants' wagons were a blur on the road, and the small conclave of fortunetellers in their bright white robes, and the troupe of bards in their colorful hats. They passed granges large and small, fields filled with cattle and goats and sheep; carved stone gateways, some grand, some simple, named each grange as they raced past it. Apiaries, too, with alternating rows of fruit trees, just beginning to shed their blooms for delicate green leaves, and thick beds of wildflowers and flowering shrubs and fragrant grasses. And vineyards, ancient vines wrapped round and round trellises that looped back and forth, back and forth.

A shepherd waved his hat, and a little girl swinging upside down from an apple tree waved her hand. A bard tipped his hand and grinned.

Ariemme waved back.

They stopped at a crossroads well, and she let the horse drink his fill. And then another hour, the sun moving slowly into the west.

And then she found herself at the Grange of the Cork Tree.

She slowed Sparrow Song to a trot, then a walk, finally stopping in the shadow of the gateway.

It was of simple design. The tall stone columns to either side, easily twice her height astride Sparrow Song, had been carved with the image of a cork tree. The plinth that formed the top of the gate had been inscribed with the name of the Grange, branches twisting in and among the words.

The path from the gate to the grange-home was short. And the house itself was relatively small; only a single level, with what might have been a sleeping loft at the back. Smooth white adobe walls, brightly painted with flowers and gryphons and bulls, and a swarm of bees around the front door. Grass and moss covered the roof, a few wild-flowers just beginning to poke out their heads. A low stone wall with a gate separated the grange-home from a grazing field off to the right, and small vegetable garden and well to the left.

A single cork tree grew there, partially shading the well.

Here. Here she would find the answers she needed. She would find the corpse of the bull, and that would lead her to the child of the Marrow Witch, and the Caretaker would be saved.

Her father.

The Pasithea, no matter the leanings of their heart, was allowed no spouse. Others could wed as they chose, but the Pasithea remained unbound, like the Maiden Herself. So it was for Ariemme's mother, and her grandfather, and all of the Pasitheas who had come before, back to the first, newly-arrived on the island chosen as their sanctuary by the Maiden.

Her mother had never forbidden Ariemme from learning more about her father; from spending time in his company, speaking with him. But such behavior had not been encouraged, either.

There is too much of him in you, and not enough of me.

Ariemme bit the inside of her lip.

No, she did not know him well. But she knew that he did not deserve to die.

She touched her heels to Sparrow Song's flanks. The horse dutifully moved forward, passing beneath the carved stone branches of the cork tree.

***

Three hours. It was now the third hour after high sun. Ariemme studied the shadow of the cork tree. Or at least very close to the third hour.

Patting Sparrow Song's neck, she swung down from his back. Her knees shook with the impact of her feet on the ground, and the sudden stillness of her muscles made her back twinge.

A quick swig from the wineskin.

Shaking her legs, Ariemme led Sparrow Song over to the well. She filled the bucket and set it in the grass. Leaving the horse to happily drink, she made her way back to the door of the grange-home.

She knocked once, twice, and again.

Somewhere, not far away, a dog barked.

Turning, she peered over the stone wall and across the field. About two dozen cattle wandered through the grasses, pulling at the tender heads or chomping on the scattered piles of hay. There were a few goats, too, and even some pigs; uncommon, but not unheard-of.

The dog barked again.

Stepping away from the door, Ariemme moved to the stone wall and set her hands on top of it. Two of the cows peered at her curiously, then went back to eating. The bull of the herd twitched his tail, eyes dark. A goat ran right up to the wall and demanded a head scratch. She obliged, her gaze sliding across the mixture of animals until it finally landed on their human caretaker.

He studied her in return, wide floppy hat with a bright blue band pulled down low to protect his face and neck. His torso was bare and dark, his skirt loose and comfortable in the spring afternoon, his boots laced high around his knees to protect his legs against the grasses and thorns and bugs and snakes. The twisted staff in his hand was plain except for the blue ribbon tied near the top, tiny golden bells dangling from its length.

Those bells tingled lightly as he moved across the field towards her. The dog followed, its tail stiff, head down.

The bull continued to watch her, eyes dark, and the goat was still demanding head scratches.

When he was close enough, Ariemme dipped her head and pressed one hand to her heart. "Vernaltide blessings, grange-keeper. May the Maiden and Her covenant hold you safe and grant you prosperity."

"And you, nymphelle. What brings you to the Grange of the Cork Tree?"

Ariemme hid a frown. His voice was familiar. And the way he held his head, the angle of his chin ….

She cleared her throat. "I come seeking information. Twin bulls were born on this grange three years past. One of the twins died. The other was taken to the Hall of the Pasithea and selected to join the herd there. Is that correct?"

The grange-keeper narrowed his eyes and gave a slow nod. "Aye, that is correct. This interests you why?"

This time, Ariemme did frown. The longer he stood before her, the more familiar he seemed. "Can you tell me what became of the corpse of the dead twin?"

His fingers tightened around his staff. The dog growled, long and low.

The goat who had been enjoying the head scratches

bleated in alarm and leaped away. The herd of cattle responded by shifting restlessly, sidling further away, and the bull snorted in warning.

"I repeat," the grange-keeper said, "why does this interest you?"

Ariemme fiddled with the bundle that held her food. "The surviving twin was chosen as the beloved Son of the Maiden. But now he has been slain. He lies dead. A curse. Malefic magic."

The grange-keeper drew in his chin and glared down at her. Frustrated. Arrogant.

That look. She knew that look.

She saw it almost every day on Tieffem's face.

The grange-keeper. The grange-keeper was Tieffem's father.

~ FOUR ~

"Nay. I am not."

Ariemme realized that she was moving backwards and stopped. "What?"

"I said that I am not. I did not lie with the Pasithea and seed her."

One of the goats bleated loudly and the grange-keeper turned away for a moment, checking the herd. The dog trotted out among the animals, head high, but was not growling. The grange-keeper nodded once and turned back to her.

"You say I am Tieffem's father. I am not. I am brother to their father. I have never laid eyes on the Heir, though I am told there is a resemblance."

"Aye. A strong one." Ariemme shifted her skin of wine. "Who told you this?"

The grange-keeper's jaw tightened. He did not answer, instead turning away again, clicking his tongue. The dog barked twice in response and trotted further out into the field, disappearing among the herd animals.

"Come," he said and lifted his hat to wave it towards

the little house. "You look as though you could use a cooling rest, and somewhere to spread your food."

With that, he moved a short distance down the wall. The gate clicked open and closed at his touch and he strode across the yard, towards the grange-home. Ariemme hesitated, then picked up her feet and followed him.

She hesitated again at the door, framed by that painted swarm of bees, pausing on the threshold and allowing her eyes to adjust to the darker interior. The grange-keeper, on the other hand, made no such allowances for the dimness; no doubt he knew his home as well as she knew her own (or at least the kitchen courtyard).

She studied the room as it became clear: a single open space with a smooth, hard-packed floor and a hearth built into the far wall. A great bull skull was mounted above the hearth, smaller bones (human and herd) strung on bright blue ribbons dangling from its horns. A table and chairs; shelves for clothes and boots and all the tools a grange-keeper might need; other shelves for scrolls and blankets and candles, bread and hard cheese and jerky. She could even make out hatches in the back corners of the floor, no doubt covering food pits dug into the ground. Colorful paintings of flowers, bulls, bees, dolphins, gryphons, and trees spread across the walls and up to the sleeping loft above the hearth, where high windows let in a bit of light.

Small, yes, but lovingly-maintained. This was a home.

Ariemme finally crossed the threshold. Lifting her wineskin and bundle of food off her shoulders, she set them on the table. "Would you join me? I would thank you for your hospitality by sharing my food with you."

He pulled off his hat, laying it on one of the shelves, and nodded. The little bells on his staff jingled as he leaned it against the wall and then lifted down some of the bread, cheese, and jerky, and a pair of clay cups.

With their feast spread across the table, he held out his hands, one facing palm up, the other palm down. Ariemme mirrored his gesture, silently echoing the blessing as he spoke it out loud.

"Maiden most gracious, we thank you for these gifts, and for the covenant that holds us safe. May we remain always true and grateful."

They sat, Ariemme tucking her feet under the chair, and for long minutes they ate in silence. Outside, she could hear the goats bleating, and the occasional *rrr-rrr-rree* of the pigs, and even Sparrow Song snorting as he loudly slurped from the bucket. The dog barked once and then fell quiet.

The birds were not quiet.

Her gift of wing-tongue was not strong, weaker than her gift of sinuous-tongue. But it was enough to understand a trill here, a warble there.

... stinky ... stinking ... rot ... foul blood ... angry trees ....

"Why are the trees angry?"

The grange-keeper choked on his wine. He carefully set aside the clay cup and leaned back in his chair. He swallowed, drawing in a long breath. Finally, he spoke. "I am Fferrieth, son of Dorra and Merri, and keeper of the Grange of the Cork Tree. I am brother of Jemmien, whom you know as the father of the Heir."

"I am Ariemme, third child of the Pasithea, and elder sister of Tieffem, the Heir of the Pasithea."

"Do you remember him? Jemmien?"

Ariemme slowly shook her head. "I do not. I was too young, and was still nursery-bound."

Fferrieth looked around the small room, eyes trailing across the shelves and paintings. "He wanted to leave here.

Near as soon as he could walk, he was off down the road. In his sixteenth year, he finally convinced our parents to allow him to travel to the City of the Hall of the Pasithea. To apprentice in a trade. A good trade." The grange-keeper shrugged. "But nothing held his attention. Cobbler, weaver, bard, courtesan, carpenter, potter." Another shrug. "He would study, practice, then grow bored and find a new trade. And so it was that he tried his hand at fortunetelling, and came to the attention of the Pasithea."

"The Autumnaltide rites." Ariemme took a quick sip of wine, remembering what she had learned of Tieffem's father from half-heard conversations, gossip, and hurried whispers. "He was among the fortunetellers invited into the Hall to bleed and read the teeth and bones for the coming year."

"Aye." Fferrieth leaned his elbows on the table. Melancholy and shame pulled at the corners of his mouth. "He caught the Pasithea's interest. Perhaps it was his face. Perhaps his prediction."

"That her next child would wear a skirt as red as hers."

"Hmm. No lie, that."

Those half-heard conversations, gossip, and hurried whispers filled her mind. The fortuneteller — Jemmien — had lain with the Pasithea only during the Autumnaltide rites. She had never sought him out again, but he had returned often to the Hall, reading for any who asked, and many who did not ask. He had made a nuisance of himself, but his predictions were so chillingly accurate, so frighteningly precise that no one had dared to send him away, not even the Pasithea. And nine moons later, on the eve of Aestvaltide — the most auspicious of days — the Pasithea had birthed Tieffem.

And Jemmien had dared to lay claim to the Pasithea and

her child. He had stormed into the Hall of the Red Throne, proclaiming that it was his prophecy and his seed that had allowed the child to be conceived. And there would be more such children, he had declared, strong in the blessings of the Maiden, worthy of red skirts, if the Pasithea would join her hand with his.

The Shield had nearly killed Jemmien for his blasphemy.

He had fled the Hall, fled the City of the Hall. What had become of him then ...?

Ariemme did not learn any of this until many years later. Such gossip would not have been spoken in the nursery. She had picked up bits of the tale here, pieces of it there; but only bits and pieces.

She wondered if Tieffem knew any of this, or if they were ignorant of their father's madness and pride.

... stinky ... stinking ... rot ... foul blood ... angry trees ....

"Did he come back here? Did he return home?"

Fferrieth refilled his cup and took a long swallow. "Not immediately. Word eventually came back to us of what had happened. My father ...." A deep sigh. "He could not bear the shame. Sickness took him within a few moons." He waved the clay cup towards the great bull skull mounted above the hearth and the bones hanging there on bright blue ribbons. "Six winters ago, Jemmien finally came home. My mother wept at the sight of him, and I nearly set the dog to drive him from the grange."

Ariemme flinched, already suspecting what Fferrieth would say.

"He wore hollowed-out bones in his hair and his tongue was stained black by marrow blood."

The flinch turned into a full body shudder.

Fferrieth opened and closed his mouth, again and then

again. He took another long swallow of wine, and finally spoke again. "I do not know when he surrendered himself to the Marrow Witch. When he swore himself as her child. I only know that when he came to us, he pledged that he had turned away from her, that he had found his way back into the grace of the Maiden."

"And you believed him."

The grange-keeper's jaw flexed. "My mother believed him. And, for a time, it seemed that her faith in him was justified. I saw no evidence of malefic magic. He removed the hollow bones from his hair. His tongue turned pink again. He watched the herd, aided in the births of calves and kids, harvested honey from wild hives in the woods." Fferrieth set down the cup, picked it up again and moved it to the other side of the table, fiddled with a chunk of hard cheese. "One year passed. Two. Three. And then late in the summer, I left, tracking a kid that had wandered out of the field and into the woods. In hindsight, I know it was deliberate. Jemmien let the kid out of the field himself. By the time I found the goat and returned to the grange, it was done."

He waved his hand at the bones again, the movement stilted and twitchy.

Ariemme peered closer. Unable to see them clearly, she rose from her chair and crossed the small room to stand before the hearth.

There were a great variety of bones: goat and pig, dog and deer. And, yes, human. A forearm bone; from his father Merri, most likely, hung from a place of honor at the tip of the right horn. And another … oh. A jawbone, on the left horn. But the teeth had been removed, and the bone itself was pitted and pockmarked.

Hollow.

Fferrieth's voice cracked. "That was all he left of her. I hung her next to my father."

Ariemme gagged and pressed a hand to her mouth.

Jemmien had murdered and harvested his own mother.

Fferrieth's voice was so low that she could barely hear it.

"He is somewhere out there. Somewhere in the woods. I looked for him. I have been hunting him for years. But I have not been able find him. Only evidence that he still lives, and that he was — is — still a child of the Marrow Witch."

"Angry trees," she whispered.

Fortuneteller. Jemmien had been a fortuneteller, one whose predications were chillingly accurate. He had still been at the grange three years past when the bulls were born. Had he foreseen the birth of the twins? The selection of one as the beloved Son of the Maiden? Had he waited, watched, plotted? And then acted?

Perhaps his mother had seen and tried to stop him. Perhaps he had planned to harvest her all along. An offering to the Marrow Witch.

Ariemme turned and found Fferrieth slumped forward in his chair, elbows resting on his knees, head down.

"Did you know that he had taken the bones of the bull? The dead twin?"

"There should have been no bones for him to take. The twin lived only a few days. It was small. I burned the corpse. It went quickly."

"Perhaps not bones, then, but something. There was something left of the twin."

Her eyes darted to the high narrow windows.

It was nearing the fourth hour past high sun. She only had until the seventh hour.

"You have failed the covenant. Had you called the Guard when your brother first returned home, your mother would have lived, the Bull would have lived, the sacrifice would have been guaranteed. And, again, if you had alerted the Guard after he slew your mother, they would have hunted him down. They would not have left the woods until his head decorated one of their spears. And for that the Maiden will hold you to account."

With every word, his head dropped further. His shoulders began to shake.

"The angry trees," she said. "You will take me to them."

Fferrieth's head snapped around. "I have not found him, not after all these seasons and years hunting him. Why do you think that you will?"

She tilted her chin up. "Because I am a daughter of the Pasithea. And the birds will show me the way."

***

They rode Sparrow Song deep into the forest. Sunlight speared down through the branches in sharp beams, scattering across the leaves and roots of the forest floor. Birds chirruped overhead and squirrels dashed madly up and down tree trunks and through the canopy.

Fferrieth was silent behind her, only directing her to steer Sparrow Song towards the northwest. He carried his staff, the ribbons and bells carefully removed and left at the grange-home, and used it to push thick shrubs or prickly thorns aside, allowing the steed safer passage.

She knew that he was leading her true. The birds high above grew increasingly agitated the deeper they rode into the forest. And the trees began to thin out, their trunks becoming narrower and narrower, with fewer buds on their branches. More sunlight poured down through the widening gaps in the canopy, heating her bare head and shoulders and chest and back.

"There." Fferrieth pointed with his walking stick.

Sparrow Song huffed unhappily and locked his legs, refusing to move any further.

Ariemme stared at the clump of trees. Twisted. Brittle grey-white with bark like ash. Lumpy roots pushed up through the ground, bleeding a blackish-red ooze.

These trees were not angry. They were of the Marrow Witch now, manifestations of her hunger.

No, it was the trees near that were angry. And afraid.

She tilted her head back, studying the canopy. After a moment, a flicker of movement caught her eyes.

A single sparrow peered down at her, eyes curious, head canted to one side.

Appropriate.

Perhaps the Maiden had a hand in the bird's appearance?

Ariemme whistled. Not well, but the bird seemed to understand her question. It responded by hopping back and forth on the branch, trilling a response.

Oak. Yelling oak? No. Shouting oak?

Frowning, frustration building in her chest, Ariemme whistled again. The sparrow hopped more rapidly, wings fluttering. It trilled the same response.

"Do you know of an oak that yells? Or shouts?"

Fferrieth's brows drew together. "There was an elm that made a strange sound when the wind struck its trunk, but it was felled by a storm a decade ago." His chin drew back and his eyes widened. "There is an oak. I remember now. We visited it when we were children hunting for honey. The knot in the trunk had the look of an open mouth and eyes, as if it were yelling."

"Where? Show me."

He lifted his walking stick, pointing over her shoulder.

Past the clump of rotted, corrupted trees, deeper into the forest.

***

The sparrow followed, chirruping wildly. It was soon joined by more sparrows, and wrens and jays and ravens and even a few owls. A mad, cacophonous congress, all of them singing and flapping their wings.

The disjointed riot of half-understood words gave Ariemme a headache.

… rotting breath … old bones … dance … backwards … shadow … stinking … screaming tree …

Fferrieth's hand lifted to her shoulder and he leaned forward. His voice was so soft that it was nearly inaudible beneath the trills and hoots and caws of the birds.

"Just there. See that elm with the hooked branch? The oak with the strange knot is but twenty paces further on."

Ariemme nodded silently, and slid from Sparrow Song's back. She patted the horse's neck and he stamped his hooves nervously.

She understood his fear.

A child of the Marrow Witch. Skilled in curses —

"I see you, my child." Loud enough to be heard over the calls and trills of the birds, frightening them into sudden silence.

— and fortunetelling.

Ariemme tried to swallow, her mouth suddenly dry. Her heart stuttered in alarm.

"Come, my child. Come. Our meeting has been many years in the making. But I have foreseen it. Yes, I have foreseen it."

Her feet were carrying her forward. Hands curled into fists at her sides, Ariemme paced slowly across the ground and around the elm with the hooked branch.

Five paces. Ten. Fifteen.

The oak appeared among the other trees, standing alone in a tiny clearing. Late afternoon sunlight dribbled down through the branches, creating a ring of green and gold around the tree.

And there, at the base of the tree, beneath the knot that looked like eyes and a screaming mouth, sat the child of the Marrow Witch.

~ FIVE ~

HIS HEAD COCKED TO ONE SIDE, THE HOLLOW BONES IN HIS HAIR clicking. His eyes narrowed. "Oh, now this is unexpected. Yes, indeed. A rare outcome, not often foreseen. The marrow most often showed my child. Tieffem. Grown proud and strong. Sometimes it showed me the Shield." His lips curled in distaste. "Sometimes an ordinary company of Guards. Even an apprentice Lorekeeper. But not often … *you*." His head cocked the other direction. "The least of the Pasithea's children."

Speak. Speak! Find your tongue!

"Yes." A whisper. She swallowed and forced the word to come out more forcefully. "Yes," she said again, then again. "Yes. I am the least of the Pasithea's children. My skirt is pink. Pale pink. It will never be red." Swallow again. Speak! "And yet it is I who found you. The least child, the least likely outcome, and *I* am here. Not Tieffem, not the Shield or Guards, not even an apprentice Lorekeeper." She lifted her chin. "Me."

The child of the Marrow Witch — Jemmien; he had a name, a plain, ordinary name — grinned, showing red-black teeth and darkened gums. So like Teiffem and even Fferrieth, yet so awfully, horribly different. "And you will do what, least of her children?"

Speak. Human-tongue.

Wing-tongue.

Sinuous-tongue ....

"A good man will die this night. An innocent." She slipped a slow, low susurrating hiss at the end of *this*. "He does[hiss-ss] not des[hiss-iss-s]erve to die. It is you who [hi-ss-ss]slew the bull, the beloved [hiss-s-s]Son of the Maiden."

"Aye. She has lost her sacrifice, so another must be made. His tongue may affirm, but his heart weeps in fear and denial." Another fierce grin. "The covenant will not hold! No! It will not! The marrow has shown me! The Maiden will turn her face away from the people, and then the land and the people will belong to the Marrow Witch!"

In the trees beyond the circle of sunlight and green, around the screaming oak, the birds were singing again. The sounds was rising; a few trills at first, then more and more. Louder. Agitated.

"And oh the glories that will grace the land! Temples of bone, altars of skulls! Whole forests to feed the fires! Babes fresh from the womb readied for sacrifice! Kin carving the bones of kin in her honor!"

From the corner of her eye, Ariemme saw the little sparrow alight on a branch over the head of the child of the Marrow Witch. The bird hopped from foot to foot, wings fluttering.

If Jemmien noticed the sparrow, or the cacophony in the trees, he gave no indication. Perhaps he did not care.

"And I — ah — your mother should have shared her

throne with me. Instead, I shall build a throne of her bones."

Find the words. Use your tongue. "The covenant will hold. I will [hiiss-ssh-ss]see to it mys[his-s-s-s]elf."

He laughed, his head tilting back. His chest shook and the hollow bones in his hair danced.

There, in the darkness of the grass beneath the trees to the right, a narrow spotted shape moved. Spotted dull green and brownish-purple; colors to hide. Barely the length of her hand, barely the width of her thumb. Ariemme dared not to look at it, her gaze fixed on the child of the Marrow Witch.

"*You*, pink skirt? *You* will ensure the covenant?" He leapt to his feet and tapped out a strange, rapid pattern on the earth. He lifted his arms, tossed his head.

With the movement, she caught the first whiff of a rotting stink. His breath, his body. She bit her tongue to hold down a gag.

More taps of his feet and he moved in a twisting, slithery circle counter to the sun.

The ground heaved.

The birds in the trees screamed and took to the air, a mad flapping of greens and blues and blacks. Only the sparrow remained, clinging to the oak. Branches and trunks creaked and groaned terribly, and Ariemme stumbled, trip-ping to her knees. The golden bees in her hair clicked wildly. Her skirt protected her legs, but her toes scraped badly. She felt the sting of blood against raw skin.

Jemmien was laughing again.

Yes. Use his name. Think of him as Jemmien, ordinary, the son of grange-keepers.

The ground heaved again. Ariemme heard the earth split somewhere behind her, and trees fell, cracking.

Sparrow Song was neighing wildly, his panicked whinnies mixing with the screams of the birds and the splintering of the trees.

Ariemme's eyes darted to the shadows to the right, hunting for that little spotted brownish-purple and dull green shape.

Nothing.

Back to Jemmien.

He stopped tapping his feet and spinning, and the ground stopped heaving. The trees continued to sway for long moments, leaves and early blossoms fluttering to the ground. They littered the forest floor and the circular, sun-lit space around the oak.

"I am a child of the Marrow Witch. The winds obey me. Fire burns at my command. I cleave the earth with a word and boil water with my breath. Blood answers my summons, and marrow shows me the shape of the world to come."

Spotted purple and green, sliding beneath leaves and petals, between blades of grass.

"What are *you*, compared to me and all that I can do?"

Speak. "I am Ariemme. Daughter of the Pasithea. Child of the Maiden. Shield of the Covenant." She stood, little golden bees jingling. "I am the least. And I am your death."

She whistled.

The sparrow dove out of the screaming oak tree, caught a strand of Jemmien's hair in its beak, pulled, flapping madly.

He lifted a hand, swatting.

The serpent struck. Tiny fangs, not even the width of her fingernail, sank into the soft skin beneath his ankle. An instant. Less than an instant. A flick of its tail and the serpent turned, gliding across the small clearing towards her.

The sparrow fluttered through the sunlight and settled on her shoulder, threads of hair still dangling from its beak.

Jemmien stood utterly still, his eyes wide. He stared at her for one heartbeat, two, three.

Ariemme crouched, extending one hand, one finger. She hissed, a soothing, thankful susurration. The serpent responded with a flick of its tongue, just grazing the tip of her finger.

In a few years, it would be as grand as the snake that the Grandfather of Serpents paraded around the Hall of the Pasithea, a vibrant green and purple. But now it was plain, well-hidden, an infant, barely hatched. And for that, all the more venomous.

Jemmien's head dropped, his gaze fixing on the two minuscule drips of blood that slid down his ankle.

The serpent flicked its tongue again and then glided away, disappearing into the darkness of the forest.

The sparrow flitted its wings, brushing the side of her neck.

Jemmien fell. He dropped to his knees. The bones in his hair rattled. And then down, his face smashing into the ground.

He was still. Still.

Ariemme pushed herself back to her feet. Her toes ached. Her knees were shaking. Her throat felt tight and dry, like she would never be able to speak again, and her head throbbed.

One cautious step and then another. She bent over slightly, studying the back of the child of — no. Jemmien's back. His unmoving back.

The venom had worked even faster than she had expected.

The sparrow trilled again, dropping the threads of hair.

"Yes, I see it," she answered. Human-tongue not wing-tongue.

Bending over further, golden bees brushing over her shoulders, she grimaced and tugged at a clump of matted hair. A flat tooth emerged, not much bigger than her thumbnail, perfect for grinding tough grasses and hay.

A bull's tooth. A tooth of the deceased twin. A neat hole had been drilled down through the center, the tooth hollowed out.

The marrow and blood and pulp had served Jemmien well. The curse he had crafted had slain the beloved Son of the Maiden, threatened to undermine the covenant, and now threatened her father's life.

So little to have wrought such damage and fear.

Ariemme tore a thin strip of fabric from the bottom of her skirt. She placed the tooth in the middle, rolled the fabric tight, and then tied the makeshift necklace around her throat. The bump of the tooth rested just above her collarbone.

A second, wider strip of cloth. One by one she pulled the bones from his matted hair, shivering, nearly gagging at the feel of that hair and those pitted bones until there were none left to mark his devotion to the Marrow Witch. She piled them all into the cloth, twisted it, knotted it, and looped it over her shoulder.

The sparrow worbled.

"Yes, please. That would ...." She switched tongues, her answer now soft whirrs and whistles. "Thank you."

Then she turned and walked away from the corpse.

***

There was no sight of either grange-keeper or horse. The ground near the elm was split deep and wide. Dozens of trees had fallen into the crevice, allowing a swath of sky to show through from above.

Her heart skipped at the thought that they might have fallen in, or been dragged down into the crevice by a tree.

But then she heard a whinny, somewhere off in the forest, and the clomp of hooves against splintered wood.

Breathing a sigh of relief, Ariemme glanced up. It was after the fifth hour now, the sky just beginning to darken as the sun wended its way towards the western ocean.

Finding a place where the crevice was not quite so wide, she took two large steps and leaped across. Another minute of walking brought her to Fferreith and Sparrow Song, the stallion whinnying in delight when she appeared.

She smiled and patted his nose.

Fferrieth cleared his throat. "It's done?"

"It is." She slipped around the side of the horse and motioned for the grange-keeper to assist; he made a cup with his hands and she hoisted herself onto Sparrow Song's back, his calluses tickling the bottom of her foot. "You may do with the corpse as you wish."

The grange-keeper huffed. "I will do nothing with it except to toss it down that hole."

Ariemme smiled grimly. "I thank you for your assistance and for the gift of your food, Fferrieth of the Grange of the Cork Tree."

"Will the Guards come for me?"

She hesitated. "I cannot say. In some matters, I do not know the Pasithea's mind well. Vernaltide blessings, grange-keeper. May the Maiden and her covenant hold you safe and grant you prosperity."

"And you, nymphelle, daughter of the Pasithea."

She touched her heels to the stallion's flanks. Sparrow Song whuffed and pranced forward. Faster and faster they wound there way back through the forest, in and out and in among the trees, over roots, beneath branches, the sky growing steadily darker. Golden bees clicked and clacked. The bird flitted from her shoulder, swooped along beside them, then returned to her shoulder again.

When at last they emerged from the woods — the lone cork tree and well and the neat little house to one side, the grazing field and flock and protective hound to the other — it was well into the fifth hour.

She leaned forward and pressed a hand to the side of the horse's thick neck. "Run, Sparrow Song. Fly like a bird."

And they ran.

***

They passed granges large and small, fields filled with cattle and goats and sheep. Apiaries, too, with alternating rows of fruit trees and thick beds of wildflowers and flowering shrubs and fragrant grasses. And vineyards, ancient vines wrapped round and round trellises that looped back and forth, back and forth.

There were few wagons, even fewer travelers on foot. Most had already reached their destination for celebrating the Vernaltide, or had returned home to their hearths to celebrate with kith and kin. A lone bard watched her with wide eyes, hopping to the edge of the road as she passed, bright hat tumbling from their head. A fortuneteller in a glowing white robe bowed low, head nearly touching the ground.

One hour.

On they ran. Past the crossroads and the well where they had rested only hours earlier. Another crossroads, and then a third. Brightly painted signs pointed in five different directions. Ariemme turned the stallion north-west, towards the City of the Hall of the Pasithea.

On they ran. Sparrow Song's breath sawed in his lungs. Sweat gathered on his back, beneath her legs. It dampened her skirt, the fabric sticking and grinding painfully against her skin. The bridle tangled, her fingers numb. His hooves clapped loudly against the gravel.

And then they were at the outskirts of the city, the little houses. And then larger buildings. Homes, bakeries, butchers, weavers. More and more buildings, more tightly packed. And there, in the center, the multi-tiered Hall of the Pasithea and, at its height, the Bull's Throne.

Up a street, turn, up another. Lights filled the windows and burned in torches lining the roads.

Sparrow Song slowed, Ariemme tugging gently on his bridle.

A mass of pilgrims filled the road ahead of them. Some carried jars of honey, others loaves of honey bread, plates of fried bull testicles and slabs of steak, necklaces of horns and teeth.

Ariemme ground her jaw.

So many people. Too many. They would never —

The sparrow warbled.

"Do you think that will work? Well." She nibbled at the inside of her lip, then nodded, decision made. "Yes."

She drew a deep breath and then let out a loud whistle. Whirrs and chirps and chirrups and caws and clicks. It was inelegant, crude. Nothing like the fine wing-tongue of the Gryphon Singers calling the seasons from the heights of the mountains.

Somewhere in the growing darkness, a corvid answered. Then an owl. More sparrows. Wrens.

Ariemme touched her heels to the stallion's side. He huffed, but pressed forward. They would reach the crowd in only a few steps ....

Then the birds came. A dozen, two dozen, three. White and brown and deep blue and brilliant red, large beaked and small, with fat wings and long wings and narrow wings. They swooped down out of the sky and from between the buildings and up the street behind her. Their wings brushed her hair and their cries filled her ears.

... the bull ... the bull ... Maiden's spring ... sun follows moon ... bones ... stinking bones ...

People exclaimed in surprise, throwing up their arms. They stumbled and fell and crawled away. More shouts, bodies retreating before Ariemme, before the Maiden's flock. Sparrow Song shoved through, further up the street, further, closer to the Hall of the Pasithea and the Bull's Throne.

Shouts ahead now, as people turned at the disturbance. They stepped aside, clearing a path.

Sparrow Song moved into a trot, his neck extended eagerly.

Run. Up the road.

Guards. The Hall. They were at the Hall.

Ariemme raised her hand, waving. The birds winged and whirled around her, swooping high and then returning to wheel in colorful circles.

The guards, wide-eyed, dipped their heads, half-knelt. The stallion pushed through the last of the crowd of pilgrims and they were through the gateway, beneath the plinth, and in the courtyard of the stables.

Sparrow Song's sides heaved. He dropped his head, too exhausted even to cross the courtyard to the drinking trough.

Ariemme leapt from his back, the little bird hopping from her shoulder to tweet in annoyance. The golden bees jingled. Breath short, she motioned a stablehand — maybe the only stablehand — to the horse's side.

"Walk him. Food. Water. I will return!"

She ran, bare feet slapping against the stones. Up a flight of stairs, down a corridor, up another flight of stairs, around a corner, up and up and up and up. She could hear the pilgrims outside, singing and chanting as the sun sank further west. Up and up and up.

The stairwell opened up above her, showing the dark sky and the first stars of Vernaltide. Her legs burned. Her lungs ached. She pushed on, up and through the opening and onto the platform-roof at the very top of the Hall of the Pasithea.

The Bull's Throne.

Great sculpted horns at the edges of the roof framed the eastern and western skies, marking the rising and setting of the sun at Vernaltide and Autumnaltide. The circular raised altar in the center, with its piles of kindling and blessed hides, marked the sun at its height on Aestvaltide and Hibernaltide.

There on that altar lay the corpse of the beloved Son of the Maiden.

The Bull had, indeed, been perfect. Spotless, deep black hide. Gracefully curved horns. Wide, velvety snout, sharp hooves, and fringed tail.

A beauty worthy of the Maiden.

At the head of the corpse stood the Pasithea, crescent moon blade in hand. She wore a grand crown shaped like a bull's head. Her torso and arms were slathered with honey, and her silken skirt was embroidered with flowers, hives, and gold and black bees. Dozens of the insects buzzed around her, darting in the light of the torches and the fading sunset. The Grandfather of Serpents, the Master of Honey, and the Lorekeeper and all of their apprentices were arrayed on her left, much as they had been in the Hall of the Red Throne. The Shield stood behind her, with Tieffem to her right.

The Caretaker knelt with his back to the Pasithea, stiff and straight, hands clenched at his back.

Ariemme inhaled, sudden fear and uncertainty making her tongue stick to the top of her mouth. Why had they all turned to stare at her? All except the Caretaker, that is, his expression fixed on the corpse. Had she shouted? Yelled?

The birds swarmed past her, still chirping and cawing and hooting, a mad cacophony. They angled across the platform, swooping through the sculpted horns on the opposite side, then back down and around again, through the second set of horns. And then away, away into the sky.

"Well, daughter?"

Ariemme's head jerked. How long had the Pasithea been speaking?

They were all still staring at her. Behind their veil, the Lorekeeper's expression was ... expectant. The Shield looked wary and alert, the Grandfather of Serpents impatient. The Master of Honey was looking back and forth between Ariemme and the Pasithea in confusion, while Tieffem appeared oddly impressed. Even the Caretaker had turned, his expression one of confusion and the slimmest hope. And the guards, too; only now did she notice them arrayed near the corners of the roof, spears planted against the stone.

Ariemme swallowed. She had faced down a child of the Marrow Witch. She could — she *would* — speak now.

"He is dead. The child of the Marrow Witch is dead."

Silence greeted her words.

The Pasithea turned, moon blade curled over one arm, silken skirts gliding over the stone, and strode towards Ariemme. Tieffem scrambled to keep up, falling into step behind their mother. The Shield followed. The Pasithea stopped a bare arm's length from Ariemme, the bees still buzzing around her.

More bees joined them, and then more. Ariemme couldn't count them all. They enveloped the Pasithea, burying her in a writhing mass of gold and black and glittering wings and blood-fizzing buzzing.

A long minute passed.

A tremendous heave, and the bees suddenly parted. In a great wave they lifted away and into the dark sky. The wave narrowed, turned into a current, a stream, and the bees were away, making for the apiaries scattered throughout the city and the farms beyond.

Massive bull crown tilted down, the Pasithea smiled at Ariemme. "Well done, daughter. Shield of the Covenant, indeed."

Tieffem blinked, eyebrows dancing.

Ariemme's mouth dropped open, then closed. She drew a deep breath and returned her mother's smile, a tentative upward curl of her lips that grew more certain when the Pasithea held out her hand. Ariemme took it and together they faced the Caretaker, the Lorekeeper, the Grandfather of Serpents, and the Master of Honey, and Tieffem, the Shield, and all of the apprentices and the guards, their spears still firmly planted against the rooftop.

"The bees have seen and heard and spoken. The child of the Marrow Witch is dead. Their body lies now deep in the earth, lost, never to be found. Their name is lost, and will be forgotten to time."

A short pause, a commanding sideways glance at Ariemme, who understood the hidden meaning in the Pasithea's words: Tieffem — the Heir — would never learn that it was their father who had threatened to destroy the covenant.

"She who is my daughter carries with her the bones that the child of the Marrow Witch harvested and corrupted. These shall be added to the sacrifice of the Bull who was murdered, the beloved Son — and thus shall the Maiden be satisfied and know that we hold true to the covenant."

Heads dipped and nodded in approval. The Lorekeeper seemed to be smiling behind their veil; they lifted one wrinkled hand and pressed it to their chest, half-bowing towards Ariemme. Tieffem raised an eyebrow, but said nothing.

The Pasithea released Ariemme's hand. Lifting the torn length of skirt from around her shoulder, Ariemme unknotted it and carefully deposited the bones next to the Bull's head. The hollowed tooth came next, source of the curse and all that remained of his twin.

Ariemme stepped away, moving to join her mother, Tieffem, and the Shield at the head of the Bull. And her father, now standing on unsteady legs.

The Caretaker licked his lips. He unclenched his hands from behind his back and carefully set one on Ariemme's shoulder. A gentle squeeze, a promise to speak later. To speak at length, she hoped. She curled her fingers through his and held on tight.

Stars burned high overhead. The sun had fallen beyond the western sea. The kindling and hides were lit, the fire rising, the light like molten gold across the black of the Bull. From the distant mountains, the sonorous chant of the Gryphon Singers joined the prayers and cheers of the pilgrims in the streets.

At her other side, Tieffem aimed a curious expression in her direction, gaze drifting down to take in her ripped and sweaty skirt. When the sparrow returned to her shoulder, trilling and fluttering, their gaze lifted again.

"Perhaps more red than pink, after all," they whispered.

"No," Ariemme whispered back. "Still a pale pink. Nothing more. And nothing less."

About the Author

Rebecca Buchanan is the editor of the Pagan literary ezine *Eternal Haunted Summer*. She has published multiple short stories, novelettes, and novellas, which she is in the process of collecting, as well as two poetry collections, with more on the way. A complete list of her publications may be found on *Eternal Haunted Summer*.

Novellas and Novelettes
The Adventure of the Faerie Coffin: Being the First Morstan and Holmes Occult Detection
Geek Witch and the Treacherous Tome of Deadly Danger: A Tale of Magical Dice, Cursed Books, and Blackberry Jam
The Maiden and the Marrow Witch: A Tale of Magic and Murder
The Secret of the Sunken Temple

Poetry
Dame Evergreen, and Other Poems of Myth, Magic, and Madness

Not a Princess, But (Yes) There Was a Pea, And Other Fairy Tales to Foment Revolution (Jackanapes Press)

Forthcoming
Asphalt Gods: A Walking the Worlds Adventure
The Ballad of the Chalice and the Blade: A Tale of Friederich the Bard
Blood, Honey, Snow: A Tale of Murder at the Edge of the World
The Bones Are Walking, And Other Pagan Urban Fantasy Tales
Eleanor Tilney and the Black Dog of Beechen Cliff: A Hidden Regency Adventure
Grandmother Granddaughter Wolf, and Other poems Fae, Fearful, and Fantastic
Jane Fairfax and the Siren of Weymouth: A Hidden Regency Adventure
Malkin: A Tale of Magic, Espionage, and Too-Curious Cats
Rueppelli and Yerik in the Great Bazaar of Repet-Yark: A Walking the Worlds Adventure
Vesta's Fire: A Tale of Roma Aeterna

www.ingramcontent.com/pod-product-compliance
Lightning Source LLC
Chambersburg PA
CBHW050613160726
48003CB00003B/1167